A FINE PASSAGE

Also by France Daigle

Real Life
1953: Chronicle of a Birth Foretold
Just Fine

A FINE PASSAGE

FRANCE DAIGLE

a novel

Translated by
Robert Majzels

First published as *Un Fin Passage* in 2001 by Les Éditions du Boréal

Published in 2002 by
House of Anansi Press Inc.
110 Spadina Ave., Suite 801
Toronto, ON, M5V 2K4
Tel. 416-363-4343
Fax 416-363-1017
www.anansi.ca

Distributed in Canada by
Publishers Group Canada
250A Carlton Street
Toronto, ON, M5A 2L1
Tel. 416-934-9900
Toll free order numbers:
Tel. 800-663-5714
Fax 800-565-3770

06 05 04 03 02 1 2 3 4 5

National Library of Canada Cataloguing in Publication

Daigle, France
[Fin passage. English]
A fine passage / France Daigle. — 1st ed.

Translation of: Un fin passage.
ISBN 0-88784-681-5

I. Title. II. Title: Fin passage. English.

PS8557.A423F5613 2002 C843'.54 C2002-904128-7
PQ3919.2.D225F5613 2002

Canada Council for the Arts Conseil des Arts du Canada

We acknowledge for their financial support of our publishing program the Canada Council for the Arts, the Ontario Arts Council, and the Government of Canada through the Book Publishing Industry Development Program (BPIDP). This book was made possible in part through the Canada Council's Translation Grants Program.

The author thanks the Canada Council for the Arts for its support of the writing of this book.

THURSDAY

Organization

CLAUDIA GAZES OUT the airplane's window at the sea of undulating white clouds below. The entire mechanism of the world seems, at this moment, smooth to her. The sun shines unimpeded over a brilliant white ocean, and the sky is nothing but the pure expression of its essential immensity.

A priest of sorts is seated next to Claudia. He rummages, for the hundredth time, through his worn travelling bag, produces a chocolate bar. He peels back the wrapping and waves the bar beneath Claudia's nose.

"Would you care for some?"

"No, thank you."

The large and abundantly bearded man pulls the bar away and snaps off a small piece.

"Sixteen?"

"Fifteen."

The generic priest, a Greek pope with a touch of something rabbinical — or is it the other way around? — bites into the chocolate. He breathes deeply as he chews. Grey hairs protrude from his small, squarish round hat. His black suit is equally grey with age.

"My name is Shimon. How about you?"

Though she would have preferred to stare out at the clouds and daydream, Claudia resigns herself to conversation.

"Claudia."

Again, the pope-rabbi offers her the bared square of chocolate.

"You're sure you don't want any, Claudia?"

"I'm sure, thank you."

He pulls the bar away and breaks off another piece.

"I certainly didn't travel alone at your age."

He ruminates, chewing.

"Although my parents and grandparents travelled quite a bit."

He leans closer, confiding: "You see, I'm Jewish."

And leaning closer, whispers: "I bear a secret."

Claudia nods politely, but she has no desire to continue this conversation. Discreetly, she shifts her head back towards the porthole.

"He is called Yahweh."

The pope-rabbi pronounces God's name as though his lungs were collapsing. Claudia, thinking perhaps he's taken ill, turns her head to look.

Shimon, content with his exhalation, continues.

"He is our God. Do you believe in God?"

Claudia shrugs. She doesn't know.

"Yahweh. You have to breathe it."

The pope-rabbi exhales the name of Yahweh a third time.

"Because God is breath. Almost nothing more than that. This is your first time on an airplane, maybe?"

"No."

The man folds the wrapper back over the remains of his chocolate bar.

"All right, I'm going to read now. I won't bother you any more."

He opens the book on his lap and begins to read. But not a minute passes before he turns again to his neighbour.

"Wisdom — this means something to you?"

Fearing what may follow, Claudia offers a hesitant yes in reply.

"Well! Well, believe it or not, I am a wise man. Have you ever seen one before?"

Claudia is on the verge of concluding that the man is slightly deranged. But how to bring an end to this conversation?

"No, I don't think so."

"Good! So now you have."

The man named Shimon casts a global eye around the cabin.

"People are beginning to sigh. This is a good sign."

And he adds, in the same confiding tone: "They are beginning to show fatigue. Sometimes, fatigue can be very beautiful, you know."

Two women are having lunch together in a crowded restaurant.

"Every Thursday, he'd throw out his used Kleenex."

She says this without looking up from her plate; she is working hard with her fork to retrieve a piece of sodden lettuce stubbornly entrenched in the dregs of vinaigrette. The other woman does not look up either; having harpooned a chunk of meat, she is busy enveloping it in sauce.

"Only on Thursdays? Who threw them out the other days? You?"

The leafy green yields at last and is taken. Clearly, her friend will never change.

"I mean, on Thursdays, he's more sure of himself. More confident. Optimistic."

"Ah! You mean he bounces back."

Silence permeates the restaurant.

"He wouldn't be a bit depressed, by any chance?"

"Depressed? No. At least, I don't think so."

Claudia is astonished to find that she's been sleeping, and she notices with equal surprise that the pope-rabbi has also dozed off. She remembers straining to stay awake while he chattered away about one thing and another. For what seemed like the longest time, she had struggled to keep up with the speaking face, but to no avail: the pope-rabbi's face faded, slipped into slow motion, or broke into jump-cuts, like in those old Hollywood movies that her parents occasionally suspend their social conscience to indulge in. In the end, the man suggested she yield to slumber.

"Go ahead. Don't worry about me. Sleep is a gift from God."

Claudia glances at her sleeping neighbour's delicate white hands. One of his fingers is clenched within the pages of a book with a nondescript black cover.

A stewardess comes down the aisle, pausing here and there to ask if everything is all right. Watching her walk away, Claudia notices, diagonally across the aisle, a man, approximately fifty years old, shift in his seat and uncross his legs. He shows no sign of reading.

In the restaurant, the two women have finished eating. A few scraps litter their plates, which they have pushed delicately aside.

"You really have no idea where he is?"

"He called twice. To see how I was doing."

"Where was he calling from?"

"I asked, but he wouldn't say. He said it made no difference."

"My God! Is he mixed up in something shady, or what?"

The woman who'd struggled with her lettuce laughs.

"Don't be silly. Of course not! That's just how he is."

Her friend sighs.

"And when is he supposed to come back?"

"I have no idea." She hesitates for a moment before speaking her mind. "Assuming he comes back at all."

And tossing her napkin on the table, the friend concludes: "I don't know how you manage."

Having uncrossed his legs, thereby slightly modifying his view, the man who shows no sign of reading continues to reflect on the fact that the names of the major planetary winds do not require capitals. Why not Trade Winds? Foehn? Sirocco? It seems to him that air currents ought to have the right to their proper identities, as do deserts, mountain ranges, and water currents. Why, indeed, should air currents deserve less recognition than those of water? Why not a Mistral and a Chinook, since we have the Agulhas and South Equatorial streams? Undeniable evidence that we treat wind with contempt: the monsoon stream — the only aquatic current not capitalized — is named after a wind current. Surely this can't be right? The man who shows no sign of reading adjusts his seat back, but without closing his eyes to sleep. At most, he hopes to be able to think differently.

Just how many major wind currents sweep across the surface of the globe? Four? Eight? A dozen? And why refuse the jet stream — a unique natural phenomenon, as far he knows — its capital letters? The man who shows no sign of reading glances up the aisle towards the front of the airplane. The passengers are quiet, and there are no on-flight personnel in sight. He toys with the idea of making his way up to the cockpit to ask the pilots if airplanes fly above or below the wind currents, but considering the surrounding torpor, this or any other sort of initiative seems impossible. A real Wednesday. Not quite death, but almost.

Knocking on the door, Hans felt something odd, a sort of premonition. "Of course. I'm sorry. I thought it was Friday. My mistake."

The woman looked him up and down.

"No, don't apologize. There's no mistake. The study of weekdays and their passage is an inexact science. As far as you're concerned, it's obviously Friday. I can see that. But what can I do? I have no choice but to follow the human timetable. Though, I admit, it doesn't always suit me either."

Hans was not expecting such a thorough explanation for what he considered merely absent-mindedness on his part.

"What people refer to as absent-mindedness doesn't exist."

Could this woman also read his mind? Hans wanted to be rid of this bizarre feeling, but, off balance, he wasn't even sure how to raise the subject of tomorrow.

"Fine. In any case, I'll come back . . . uh, tomorrow?"

"That's right. Tomorrow."

And without further ado, the woman closed the door.

Once, when they were famished after making love, the man who showed no sign of reading made sandwiches, which they began to eat in silence. Probably it was an ambiguous silence. And though she hesitated, in the end she had not been able to resist asking.

"What are you thinking?"

At the time, she still expected his answers to be tinged with sweetness.

"I was thinking of salt. I'm sure I put enough, but I don't taste it at all. I wonder if salt loses its taste, goes stale over time."

She was stunned; they finished their snack in silence.

Several rows behind, in a seat by the other side of the sky, Carmen is also looking through the porthole. Beside her, Terry is engrossed in an American bestseller he picked up at the airport.

"The thing I enjoyed about smoking was that feeling you got, maybe twenty-odd times a day, that you were coming to the end of something."

Terry stops reading.

"Hmm . . . I'm sure I know just what you mean, I do."

Carmen and Terry quit smoking two weeks ago.

"It's not so bad, though, eh?"

"It's bad enough."

But the man who shows no sign of reading is not always preoccupied by such superficial considerations as the freshness of salt or the status of air currents in the minds of professors of geography and orthography. Often he thinks of nothing in particular, finds himself unable to take hold of any specific thing in life's continuous flow of events. In his life's flow, that is. Of these past few months in particular, he has retained very little. Except for that Gabriel Pierné score, *Prelude and Fughetta for Wind Septet*, which fell into his hands . . . by chance. What was it that had moved him, at that instant, about two flutes, an oboe, a clarinet, an English horn, and two bassoons? Were he a musician, which he is not, the question would not have arisen. Perhaps it was the visual graphic of the score that enticed him — a painter's old reflex — but what were the chances he would undertake another painting in this life? That question was left unanswered.

"Many people pray without knowing it."

Now that Claudia understands that the pope-rabbi is not the least bit embarrassed about talking to himself, she leaves him to his monologue and continues to drift among the gentle clouds.

"Joy is the most beautiful prayer, don't you think?"

Unable to pretend any longer that she doesn't hear him, Claudia turns to her neighbour.

"Simple joys are already luminous in and by themselves, so imagine boundless joy."

To paint. What a joke! It had all begun with a ludicrous idea. Apparently, one day an uncle of his mother's, an old uncle he'd never met — sometimes he wonders if there really was such an uncle — abandoned wife, kids, and worldly goods and exiled himself to Vancouver, Canada. He was a child when they told him this family epic, neglecting to specify that the name of the tale's mythic land was spelled V-a-n-c-o-u-v-e-r, and not V-e-n-t C-o-u-v-e-r-t, meaning "covered wind" in French, as he had imagined. How many times had he tried to picture what a covered wind was like, not to mention a city of that name? Only effects of colour came to mind, the kind of effects that seemed increasingly to occur to him whenever he found himself confronted by concepts that were relatively abstract or downright unfathomable.

To paint. To this day, he cannot quite believe that this way of apprehending the world — this way of spending, or wasting, one's time — has actually allowed him to earn a living. What luck, and what a scandal! And what a relief to think that all that is more or less finished. A few traces of that past continue to tinge the edges of the life of the man who shows no sign of reading, but they do not weigh heavily in the balance. That Pierné score, for example. So tenuous, almost completely incorporeal.

Strange how, even in death, I seem to be swimming against life's current. Here, in the suicides' wing, no one is trying to come back to life. They are all precise suicides.

They have nothing more to do with the living. Oh, from time to time, I may come across a faint ray of melancholy, an evanescent memory in a glance, but none of that lasts long. Precise suicides don't struggle with such things. They're done with struggling.

The man who shows no sign of reading is well aware that his desire to give proper names to the warm, caressing winds of the planet springs from his dislike for the cold. To tell the truth, the man who shows no sign of reading has a kind of aversion to all things that appear difficult.

"... so imagine boundless joy."

In this fragment of a phrase, the man who shows no sign of reading recognizes the voice he heard earlier coming from one or two rows behind. Until now, he'd paid it no mind; it was merely part of the general murmur of the flight. The voice continues:

"Can you imagine boundless joy?"

The man who shows no sign of reading hears a younger voice reply in the negative.

"Of course, it's not easy to imagine. But at times, we get a taste of it. You'll see."

The man who shows no sign of reading is tempted to turn around. At last, some entertainment. To make the most of it, he decides to make his way to the washroom. By chance, he gets up at the same moment as the girl who is seated next to the pope — or rabbi, he can't tell which — to whom he attributes the inspired phrase. The man who'd shown no sign of reading allows the girl to go first. They proceed in single file towards the rear of the airplane, both of them feeling they are going against the current.

You've taken up your model cars again. A fine idea. But it does worry your mother to see you re-enacting the sort of collision in which I died. Of course, you can't help it. You're not sure what happened exactly, but you've heard things. You suspect — maybe it's something you overheard — that I may have done it on purpose, that I caused the accident as a way of getting out of life. How can I make you understand, my son, that I'm not a suicide? Or only to a very limited degree.

Like everyone else, I had wanted once or twice to die. Well, perhaps more than once or twice. Dying, after all, is also part of life. Sometimes I suffered terribly from a lack — a lack of perspective that would have allowed me to get out of myself, to escape my limits. I experienced this as a kind of imprisonment, as though I was enclosed inside an airplane in mid-flight. I accepted to live my life this way, though I occasionally deplored it. But how to explain to you, my son, that I am an involuntary suicide, an imprecise suicide? That the intention to die that has been attributed to me is a mistake? In any case, I would never have chosen to die on a Thursday.

All the washrooms are taken when Claudia, followed by the man who'd shown no sign of reading, arrives. But no one else is waiting, aside from, perhaps, a young man standing there, his head lowered, with an ear almost glued to one of the doors.

Claudia and the man who'd shown no sign of reading can hear someone throwing up in the washroom. The young man seems anxious.

"Carmen?"

In reply, he is greeted with another heave.

"Carmen? You all right, then?"

No reply. The young man raises his head, looks at the girl and the man, his witnesses. Worried but powerless, Terry shrugs and offers by way of explanation:

"She's preggers."

TUESDAY

Attack

HANS IS BEGINNING to like the man standing before him, a sort of cowboy of the vineyards who doesn't bother with niceties in order to spare people's feelings.

"So are you ever going to finish that jigsaw puzzle?"

It's the second time Hans has crossed paths with this man at a wine tasting, and he has no qualms about responding in an equally direct manner.

"It seems to torment you as much as it does me."

A pretty hostess passes again with wine. Both men take new glasses. At which point a small, inexplicable group movement occurs, and Hans wonders if the ground is not once more beginning to shake, a sensation he has found surprisingly pleasant since coming to live in California.

And yet, when he decided to come to San Francisco, Hans had not even thought about the famed San Andreas fault. He had never, in his entire life, been the least bit concerned about earthquakes. Now that he has experienced them several times, he's taken a liking to these underground rumblings. They shake him up in a new and intensely intimate manner, as though some sort of primordial coherence was being awakened in him.

The two women are the last remaining customers in the dining area of the small restaurant.

"And how's work?"

"Bah. They decided people want to reread Balzac, so we're doing Balzac all over again. But we're almost done."

"And then what?"

"Gorky."

The woman who'd struggled with her lettuce draws a cigarette from her pack and lights it.

"I've got to go after this."

"I thought you'd quit smoking."

The woman exhales her smoke, nodding her head in a way that signifies neither yes nor no, before adding:

"I smoke only in public."

When he bought this second jigsaw puzzle, Hans was under the spell of a minor Tuesday psychosis: he was feeling particularly courageous, Plutonian, Chinese. He had already completed a reproduction of the *Census at Bethlehem* by Bruegel the Elder when he came upon this *Winter Landscape* by the artist's youngest son, Jon, known as Velvet Brueghel. This one was also a three-thousand-piece puzzle; it depicted a number of small figures engaged in various activities on the outskirts of a snowy Flemish village. On a door that served as a table in a corner of his large rented room, Hans had successfully assembled the outer edge of this second jigsaw, but he had barely begun to work on the interior. Something was stopping him from going any further. It had been like that for weeks now.

"There's something in that puzzle beckoning to you, but you won't give in to it."

Hans had sought among the people around him someone whom he could truly look up to as wise.

"Maybe you just don't want to finish it. To be done with it."

As he was paying, Hans had noticed that the skin around the woman's fingernails had been chewed up. It made him feel strange. And yet, she had been highly recommended.

Terry and Carmen are in line to go through customs. The line they chose moves forward at more or less the same pace as the others. No one seems to havc any emotions. Terry and Carmen step forward to the counter together. The official does not take kindly to this infringement of the regulations.

"One at a time."

He gives a cursory nod towards the waiting line. Terry understands that one of them must retreat behind the line traced on the ground. This does not seem possible to him, and he attempts to explain it to the man before him.

"She's preggers."

The officer understands the word, but he's not immediately sure what he is meant to apply it to. He raises his head, sees the young man's eyes brimming with sincerity, then sees the young woman, who looks like a homesick schoolgirl. He chooses not to give himself any trouble, pretends to understand, checks their passports, returns them, and lets the couple pass without asking any questions.

Terry and Carmen pick up their luggage and make their way to the taxi stand, where yet another line awaits them. Terry did not expect things to be so organized. When it's their turn, he pushes the bags up to the trunk of the cab and even tries to put them in. This does not appear to please the driver, who is in a less-than-cheerful mood. Terry feels compelled to explain why he is doing all the work himself, without Carmen's help.

"On account of she's preggers, see."

The driver takes not the slightest notice of what's being said, instead shoving the last of the suitcases into the trunk and muttering all the while into his moustache. The two travellers realize this is no place to dawdle; they get into the super-clean BMW. Terry pronounces as clearly as he can the name and address of the small hotel a friend recommended. Unable to understand, even after he's made Terry repeat it several times, the driver asks to read the address scrawled on the paper, which turns out not to be all that clear either. Nevertheless, in the end, the cab does make its way into the heart of Paris.

Here, in the wing for precise suicides, they laugh at me a little. As far as they're concerned, there's been no mistake. I quickly realized how useless it was to try to convince them of the contrary. At first, from time to time, they listened to me — out of a kind of charitable spirit I haven't been able to figure out — but I could see my appeal was falling on deaf ears. It was written in their postures, in their immobility. It is impossible to describe just how completely they have ceased to live.

It may seem somewhat contradictory to see them as entirely dead, on the one hand, and then to feel that they are laughing at me, or that they are capable of charitable feelings. And yet that's how it is. But instead of reassuring me, these slight infringements on the rules of death only increase my feeling of solitude, my inability to join them. I never believed much in heaven and hell, but if I were to imagine them for a few moments, what I've just described would be pretty close to hell. There's something unbearable about this gnawing feeling of not being where I belong. On the other hand, I can see that lots of people on earth suffer for much the same reason.

Claudia must wait almost ten hours in the airport before embarking on the second phase of her journey, which will take her to her destination. She will join her parents on their kibbutz in Israel, for an unofficial holiday — her college's policy on holidays being rather liberal. The goal of the vacation is of course to reassure her parents of her well-being, and to help them feel right about their own choices.

These trips are nothing new to Claudia. For several

years now, her parents have been unable to live without a cause. Which is what she explained to the pope-rabbi, because even though he was a bit odd, Claudia sensed that he wished her well.

"At least they're not a pain in the butt, right?"

The pope-rabbi's reaction made her laugh, because Claudia does indeed feel rather lucky that her parents have decided to leave the nest. And though she doesn't mind seeing them once or twice a year, a single week at a time rather than two would be quite sufficient. She can see herself in them, but within a few days, she always ends up feeling that this particular natural resource is non-renewable.

The pope-rabbi was reassuring.

"We must be dead to one's parents, you know. It is written thus, so don't worry about it."

And he turned back to his book.

The woman who smokes only in public is quietly enjoying her cigarette. Her friend, meanwhile, leapfrogs from one thought to another.

"Do you know if he's painting at least?"

"Oh, I doubt it. I don't know. He hasn't said anything about it."

"He's wasting his talent."

The idea that talent is something someone can waste seems suddenly odd to the woman who smokes. She could debate it, but today she lacks the energy to tilt against clichés. Not all Tuesdays are alike.

Her friend switches topics.

"Someone's moved in next door. The movers were in yesterday. There wasn't a single piece went in that house that wasn't gorgeous."

And in conclusion:

"You should quit smoking. You're racing to an early grave."

The woman who smokes crushes her cigarette butt in the ashtray.

"Funny, I feel as though I'm calmly walking towards it."

Terry and Carmen have piled their suitcases as efficiently as possible in the small space of their room. They have also pushed the two single beds together. Carmen is in the bathroom washing up. And talking to Terry. She's always enjoyed talking to him like this — he in the bedroom and she in the bathroom.

"You don't have to go telling everyone I'm pregnant. Doesn't even show."

It's as though the intervening walls allow each of them to take a firmer stand.

"Well, that's the whole point, isn't it! How else are they going to know, then?"

"They don't need to know, do they? Makes no difference."

Terry's answer is not immediate.

"Well, I'm thinking it does make a difference."

And he adds, as he struggles to open the window: "Seems to me it's my way of being preggers along with you."

Carmen finds the answer sweet; she can think of nothing to add. She continues applying her makeup.

"Are we Tuesday or Wednesday, then? I'm all muddled."

"Makes no difference. Tuesday, Wednesday . . ."

When she comes out of the bathroom, Terry is stretched across the bed, trying to touch the opposite walls of the room with the tips of his fingers and toes and succeeding.

What drew Hans's gaze to this particular puzzle was the somewhat dilapidated windmill about halfway up the painting and slightly to the left of centre. The way the mill sits on a base of pillars and piles gives the impression that the wind not only turns the vanes but rocks the whole structure. In spite of the great number of other buildings in the painting, this is the only windmill. It sits alongside a frozen river, on which people seem to be strolling quite happily. Strangely, it was as though Hans was seeing this landscape for the first time. As though he hadn't lived all his life in the Netherlands.

Meandering along the corridors of the airport lounge, the man who'd shown no sign of reading is not surprised to find large paintings hanging on the walls. It has become general practice to hang art in this sort of place — inoffensive art, of course, but colours just the same; never entirely without effect.

The man has long ago lost the habit of pausing to admire such decorations, moving steadily along instead, though with no purpose other than to pass the time. Wandering in this way, he comes upon Claudia seated in front of a wall of windows, looking out over the landing strip, her back to a painting of intermingled blues and greens. As though by pure chance — the man who'd shown no sign of reading is forever being swept along by pure chance, in which he only half believes — Claudia turns her head at that very moment and their eyes meet. For a fraction of a second, he is gripped by how impossible it is for a man of his age to approach a young girl in this way, simply to talk to her as a man of his age. It's as though he could draw no strength at all from all his years.

It's a bit in Terry's nature to be caught in between things. Between Tuesday and Wednesday, for example; beyond the aggression and tension of Tuesday, but short of Wednesday's deliverance, short of any strict requirement.

"I mean, it's not as though we'd been here before and knew there were things you do on Tuesday rather than Wednesday, now is it?"

Still stretched across the bed, Terry is examining the room's ceiling and discovering nothing in particular there.

"I suppose we might go out and walk, or just to bed. Aren't you a bit weary, then?"

"Even if I was weary, I couldn't sleep, could I? I'm too wound up, is what it is. I wouldn't mind a coffee, though."

Terry springs to his feet, happy to proclaim his fine mood.

"If it's a coffee you're wanting, sweetie, a coffee is what you'll get."

With that, he pulls his toiletries bag from under the bed — having found no space in the bathroom for it — and takes his turn in the tiny washroom. Nor does Carmen despise talking to him this way, from the bedroom to the washroom.

"We should go to the Marais."

"*Marais*, as in 'swamp'?"

"It's a neighbourhood full of artists. With real narrow streets."

"And what's so swampy about that that they have to call it the Marais?"

"Don't know, do I? It must have been a swamp before."

"Before what?"

"Before before. Can't you hurry up? I'm dying to get out."

Terry finishes brushing his teeth and emerges from the bathroom.

"I love you, sweetie."

"I love you too. Now get moving, will you."

The man who'd shown no sign of reading feels that the airport is a sort of universal place, so, not wishing to appear out of place, he attempts a universal approach. He selects a seat not too far from the young girl, making sure to offer a discreet greeting. Claudia returns his nod politely. He does not see how he might do more. Should he barge right in? He wishes he knew a way to proceed that wasn't too awkward. He can think of nothing. Then:

"You're not a musician, by any chance?"

Claudia takes some pleasure in the man's addressing her as an adult. The pope-rabbi had done the same, and that had pleased her too.

"No."

Not easy. She barely smiled.

"Nor am I."

The man who'd shown no sign of reading believes all is lost. Something is just not going to happen; he can feel it.

"It's odd the way sometimes something simply doesn't happen."

Claudia hears the words, but she's completely at a loss. It's the sort of phrase that either clicks or immediately turns the other person off.

"Excuse me?"

"Are you hungry? We could have a bite to eat together."

To his astonishment, the girl gets up and grabs her bag.

"Okay."

"You don't play a wind instrument? How odd. I was sure you did."

Hans tried not to be put off by the psychotherapist's New Age approach.

"Many people come to California because they can't think of any other place to go. It can be an act of hope, or of desperation. A successful completion, or a last rampart. It's something typically American. You're not an American?"

Without waiting for a reply, the woman turned to the large window overlooking the bay and the cities on the opposite shore.

"San Franciscans believe they invented the bay window. They spell 'Bay window' with a capital *B*. They also dislike Oakland a great deal. What about your dislikes?"

This woman was on the verge of creating one, but Hans resisted the temptation to tell her so.

"The end of the continent gives them a sense of freedom, lightness, renewal. Invisibility too, sometimes. Disappearance. Are you attracted to the San Andreas fault?"

The woman slipped in her questions now and then, in the midst of her monologue, without leaving time for answers. Hans decided it had to be a kind of general presentation of the themes to which they would be returning in more depth later, as they went along.

"You're not answering my questions. Are they too brutal?"

The woman looked him squarely in the eye.

"The trams here travel at nine miles an hour, and San

Franciscans are all in agreement to keep them. The 1906 earthquake came crashing in at more than seven thousand miles an hour and destroyed everything. Which means that slowness has its advantages. But beware! Speed can strike blindly. The line between serenity and indifference is a thin one."

FRIDAY

Love

TODAY CLAUDIA HAS all the time in the world to explore the area. During the first few days of her visit, she was mostly busy catching up and chatting with her parents. All three now seem sated as far as that activity is concerned, an activity that consists of reassuring one another that everything is fine and that everybody can continue living their lives as they please. She'll take advantage of this free day to mail the letter given her by the man who'd shown no sign of reading.

"I wonder if I might ask you for a small favour?"

No objection from Claudia.

"I'd like to send word to a woman. I too planned to go to Israel today, but I've just now changed my mind. Nevertheless, I would like her to think I was in Israel."

This idea struck Claudia as rather odd, even worthy of suspicion. A number of questions came to mind.

"I know it seems bizarre. But I love this woman, and I would never do anything to harm her."

Claudia decided she had no cause for restraint.

"You love this woman, and you're lying to her?"

"I'm not lying to her. I'm providing dreams for her."

"Ah, it's you. I didn't expect you to come back."

Indeed, Hans had considered putting a stop to the therapy.

"Let's talk about the fault, if you like."

But Hans immediately knows that she will do most of the talking. He's not mistaken.

"You know, of course, that couples can drift apart much as continents do."

She stares at him intensely. Hans wonders if she expects him to comment. Nothing occurs to him.

"Have you ever been in love?"

To this Hans could reply, but the woman has gone on without waiting. If he took all this seriously, he'd think he was in the middle of a novel by Kafka.

"Falling in love is in fact no more than a predisposition. The falling is really all there is to it. You see what I mean?"

Pressing her right hand on the desk, the woman swivels around in her chair to contemplate the view in the Bay window — with a capital *B*, because Hans is beginning to feel like a San Franciscan. It is at this point that he notices that two of the woman's fingers are wrapped in Band-Aids at the base of the nail. Clearly, he thinks, something's eating her. The woman turns back towards him.

"Many people leap into love as they might leap into the fault, in the hope that it will seal up again and enclose them. To be engulfed seems desirable to them. Do you think they just don't know any better? Don't answer. Answers are always wrong on Fridays. On Fridays our defences kick in."

Hans thinks he will probably get nothing out of this so-called analysis except a bit of entertainment, which is something.

"Have you wandered around the Tenderloin district? A feeling of lack seems to arise spontaneously, don't you find?"

And the woman glances nonchalantly at her watch, as though the time was passing too slowly.

"Some people choose to live on the fault, you know. They move into brand-new houses, knowing full well. For some it's an abstraction, but for others it's very real. For them, every day is a gain. In this way, they end up feeling they lack for nothing. It's the same in love. There are those who win by making sure everything is lost from the start."

In the end, when Hans tries to pay her, the woman with the chewed-up cuticles refuses to take his money.

"No, not today. Give it to the panhandlers instead. Some days it's best to steer clear of all financial considerations."

Having affixed the stamp, Claudia pauses and, for the first time, looks with curiosity at the envelope she agreed to mail for the man who'd shown no sign of reading. She turns it this way and that. Although she knows the contents — the man had quite naturally let her read the note he was sending this woman — Claudia wonders if it isn't some sort of coded message, if this man who claims to be a painter isn't really a spy or something like that.

"Ex-painter, to be precise. But I still have some paintings

on the market. They're priced too high, but what can you do?"

He also told her his name, but in passing, and Claudia had not found it useful to remember it. In any case, he really seemed to love this woman. He sealed the envelope gently and slowly.

"You really don't miss your parents?"

The question took Claudia by surprise. Now she wonders why.

"I'm sorry. I'm being indiscreet. I overheard your conversation with your neighbour in the plane, that pope."

Claudia had no idea what to say. The man, sensing that the conversation was perhaps on the verge of collapse, tried to put her at ease.

"Forget it. It doesn't matter. I can be very clumsy sometimes."

They sat for a while, allowing themselves to be rocked by the comings and goings of the people in the restaurant. Until Claudia decided to break the silence.

"And you? You don't miss her?"

The man took his time answering, but in the end, he said: "Missing is the opposite of dreaming."

And with those words, he had handed the envelope to Claudia.

Terry is a bit peeved.

"Well, if you're wanting to be rid of me, you've only to say so."

"Geez, and aren't you the great romantic."

"And what, if I may ask, is so romantic in that?"

"I'm only saying that if we were to lose one another, in the subway or some such place, instead of searching and not knowing where we were, we ought to just get on with our day alone. Each of us on our own. And I could buy you a small present, and you might do the same for me."

Terry really can't see the use of pretending to get lost.

"Well, the way you're talking, sounds like you want us to plan to go and lose each other. We may as well decide to spend the day each on our own, if that's what you want."

Carmen had not thought of it quite that way.

"Seems to me, it'd be more exciting if we were to lose each other. Not on purpose. That way, we wouldn't be expecting it. It'd be more of a muddle that way."

Terry doesn't immediately reply, but the idea has already begun to spin wheels within. Finally, he proposes a kind of compromise.

"I don't want to lose you. But if it happens, we'll do like you say."

Carmen turns in the bed, kisses him.

"I love you."

"So do I, love you. What do you think? But don't go forgetting you're preggers. That thing's half me, you know."

The restaurant had become quiet. The waitress even had time to come over and ask them if everything was fine. Everything was fine.

"He caught my attention when he spoke about boundless joy. I'd never heard that expression before. Interesting concept, don't you think?"

Claudia enjoyed listening to him talk, but his questions were often perplexing.

"I don't know. Is it religious?"

The man shrugged. "It could be, but it wouldn't have to be, I suppose."

"I don't practise any religion."

"Neither do I. But from time to time, I walk into a church. Or a temple. Or a mosque. To rest when I've been walking a lot."

Claudia felt she could fall in love with a man like this. In fact, she wondered if she had not already fallen.

"Do you have any children?"

"No."

"You didn't want any?"

"Not particularly. I wasn't against it, but it never happened. Now I don't know."

The man continues unnecessarily to stir his coffee.

"People have begun to say my paintings are my offspring."

He removes the spoon from his cup and places it in the saucer, shrugs.

"It's useless to fight against that sort of idea. And you? Do you want children?"

"I don't know."

"You have a friend? A boyfriend, I mean."

"No."

Another silence followed, and once again, Claudia was

able to break it. The ease with which she was able to break this man's silences amazed her.

"I did notice you on the plane. From the side. You showed no sign of reading."

My wife. Yes, even from this hell in which I find myself, I dare to continue calling you that, even though you feel betrayed. The days pass, but your anger does not wane. You make every effort not to let it show in front of our son. And yet you know very well that sooner or later, you will no longer be able to restrain yourself.

I don't know where I found the strength to confess to you that I had a lover. I knew you did not suspect at all. The circumstances of our life allowed me to hide the affair from you. Your absolute confidence in us, in me, made things all too easy.

At first, I was sure it would be a passing fling. A minor glitch. A detour necessary for some reason or other. I felt as though I was experiencing something of no importance, that took nothing away from you. And for that reason, it seemed better not to say anything than to upset you unnecessarily. From one time to the next, I imagined myself putting an end to it, and then, from one time to the next, I couldn't quite do it.

You know that I was coming from her place when I had the accident. That time too, I had every intention of putting an end to it. And again I had not done so. If I had broken it off and then had that stupid accident anyway, she would certainly have told you. She would have had the heart to tell you that, in the end, it was you I chose. That might have afforded you some small comfort. But it didn't happen, because once again that day, I failed to put an end to my bewitchment.

You think I committed suicide to avoid that choice. You think I was that much of a coward. I'd like to think it isn't so. I'd like to think I would have ended up doing the right thing and let you know, deep inside, that it was you I cared for above everyone else. That did not happen either. And today you don't know — and you may never know — that it's in you, and through you, that I wanted to live.

The woman who smokes only in public manages to drag herself out of her sleep. Although she went to bed early last night, she feels quite lazy. She gets up anyway and starts the morning routine that will eventually set her day in motion.

She can tell, however, in all the little things, that she is not her usual self. Objects — a spoon, the cap of a jar of cream, her apartment keys — slip through her fingers and, as though that was not enough, disappear into unreachable corners, requiring strength and contortions to be retrieved. Not to mention, they are making her late, because the morning routine, timed to the second, leaves little room for the unexpected and tolerates not even the tiniest obstacle.

As she manages, with the help of an old wooden yardstick, to retrieve her key chain and several dust bunnies that have attached themselves to it, the woman realizes that she never used to lose patience over such minutiae. She thinks of the time when they still lived together, how he made her life difficult in a thousand little ways and yet she never complained. In fact, that was one of the things she liked about their life together, that knack he had for blurring the edges of the quotidian.

Terry can't sleep. He's thinking about how he would occupy his day if ever, one fine morning, Carmen gave him the slip in Paris. He decides that what he'd like most would be to hang around in the cafés, a bit the way he does in Moncton. The Paris of famous sites, museums, and churches holds little attraction for him. He feels no need to improve himself in that way. He would also take the time to send some postcards, in particular to his father, who had lent him part of the money for the trip. Having heard that travel is the best education for the young, the master body mechanic did not want to deprive his son of just such a profitable experience, although he often had cause to criticize the boy's irresponsible lifestyle. Recently, however, the old man found that his youngest was taking life a little more seriously.

"You mean to say you didn't tell him I was pregnant?" Carmen couldn't believe it.

"What was the use of getting him all bollixed?"

"He might not have lent you the money."

Terry shrugs.

"He's got plenty of money."

"Well, anyway, all I'm saying is you could have told him. That way, at least you would've been honest."

"All right, all right, then. I'll write him."

". . ."

". . ."

"Especially when you can't stop telling everybody else and his uncle."

". . ."

". . ."

"It's not the same thing. 'Round here they don't know us, do they?"

"You don't talk much about yourself."

Claudia was just thinking how open he was about himself. Without his having said much, she felt she already had a pretty clear picture of his life. Not in the details — and perhaps in the details she would not find him so attractive — but at least she had a general idea. She liked this man.

"I haven't much to say."

"I understand. Nor do I, when it comes down to it, have much to say. The longer it goes, the more I have the feeling that life repeats itself, and the less I have to say about it."

A woman walks by their table followed by a whimpering boy. The woman is clearly at the end of her rope. So is the boy.

"See what I mean? There are always mothers at the end of their rope and kids whimpering. It's perfectly legitimate and so sad. And there's not much we can do about it. We must be patient. Life is good for that, for exercising one's patience."

The child is crying louder now. His mother is unable to quiet him. Nothing, neither firmness nor gentleness, seems to work. The man watches discreetly.

"I've half a mind to go over there and try to distract them. Mother and child both. It might change the dynamics."

"Why not? Go ahead."

The man rises, approaches the table, says something to the mother, who initially looks slightly hostile but softens bit by bit. Claudia can't hear what is being said. The child, as he watches the man speaking to his mother, gradually calms down. The man who'd shown no sign of reading now addresses the boy. The child doesn't answer, but he is listening.

To live. But what is living? Since that accident — but what is an accident? — I've lost all capacity to understand it. Death truly puts an end to so many things. Do you remember that trip we took to Labrador? It was early in our marriage, when everything was still possible. Remember the day we walked for hours along the river? We felt perfectly happy in the midst of nature, so sure of itself, so much larger than anything. Do you remember the first salmon we saw jump out of the river on its way upstream? We were thrilled. And then a second one jumped, and another. Each time you squeezed my hand harder, and each time I would have wanted to be that salmon for you, forever swimming against the current towards you.

I'm not really sure why I bring up that memory. Maybe because, here in the wing for precise suicides, nothing swims upstream any more, nothing struggles, nothing wants anything. All wanting abolishes itself.

Terry awakens after several hours of deep sleep. The idea that had kept him awake for a long time — the idea, eventually, of beating Carmen at her own game — remains with him.

At breakfast, they discuss their plans for the day. They decide to go up to the area around Montmartre, where they haven't been yet. They bend over the subway map, figure out their route, and set out. The weather is fine; the sun warms their faces.

Since the subway is not packed, Terry and Carmen can sit together. They observe the comings and goings of the people at each stop. Terry tries hard to seem perfectly calm, but inside he's ablaze with impatience. Then, at a station of no particular interest, just before the doors of the car close, he leaps to his feet, plants a quick kiss on Carmen's cheek, and steps out onto the platform, where he waves and smiles tenderly at a rapidly vanishing Carmen. He can see from her expression that she did not expect him to take the lead in this thing, but then she laughs and blows him a kiss, which warms his heart. He waits for the subway to be swallowed up in the tunnel then turns towards the escalator.

At work, it takes the woman who smokes only in public a good hour to regain her composure. She's constantly reversing letters on her keyboard, a minor morning dyslexia that doesn't surprise her, since she seems to have floated in to work rather than arrived there by her usual means of transportation. And yet, by the time she stops for lunch, she realizes she's completely shaken off her sleepwalking state and accomplished far more work than she would have thought herself capable. In the neighbourhood restaurant where she likes to eat on Fridays, it takes her a good twenty minutes to emerge from her state of extreme concentration and get back to normal. Relieved not to have made a lunch date, she takes advantage of the break to clear her head.

She returns to work after lunch with the idea of coasting through the last hours of her week. She has already decided to turn down any Friday afternoon invitations to have a drink with colleagues. She'll go straight home, pour a glass of wine, and take her time nibbling on some leftovers and watching television programs taped during the week. Finally, brushing her teeth before bed, she'll try once again to convince herself that she's not becoming completely anti-social.

After emerging from the subway, Terry walks for a solid quarter of an hour before stopping in a café. He watches the local fauna a long time and tops up on second-hand smoke before working up the courage to inquire how to go about telephoning his father. Just before falling asleep in the wee hours of the morning, he had decided to phone rather than write. His decision still holds firm.

The procedure turns out to be less complicated than he imagined, and before he knows it, he hears the voice of his father on the other end of the line.

"Dad?"

"Terry! Where are you?"

"Paris!"

"Is there something the matter, then?"

"No, no, everything's just fine. Only, there was something I wanted to tell you."

Terry hesitates a moment, unsure how to go on. This gives his father time to worry.

"Well, then, what's going on?"

"Well, I . . . I love Carmen."

His father, not understanding, waits for more. But there seems to be no more. He thinks maybe they've been cut off.

"Hello?"

"I hear you all right, Dad."

"Is it to tell me that, you're calling, then?"

"Well . . . it's . . . she's preggers."

"Already?"

"I mean, she was before we left. Pregnant, I mean."

"And is it yours?"

"Well, yeah, of course. What do you think!"

Another moment passes while neither father nor son knows what to say. Then Terry makes an effort.

"Carmen thinks I should have told you before. On account of the money."

"And what money is that?"

"The money you lent me. For the trip. Does it make a difference? For the money, I mean?"

"Will the two of you be getting married, then?"

"I don't know. We've not talked about it. Well, I suppose she might be wanting to get married."

Third brief silence. And yet, Terry feels strong enough to go on.

"Well, you won't have to pay for that. We'll make do. Is Mum there?"

"She's gone to Mass."

"You'll tell her, then?"

"How long's it been?"

"Near three months."

As his father is silent, Terry decides to lean a bit on Carmen.

"She had a bit of the sicks in the beginning, but she's a whole lot better now."

"She big yet?"

"Naw. Hardly shows, really."

Terry senses it may not be particularly useful to prolong the conversation.

"Dad?"

"What?"

"Will you be all right, then? I mean, until Mum gets back?"

Having addressed the envelope to the woman he said he loved, the man who'd shown no sign of reading was returning his pen to his jacket pocket when he changed his mind.

"I'd like to give it to you, if you like. As a kind of souvenir."

Claudia took the pen the man was offering and examined it. It was heavier than it looked.

"Okay."

Claudia is now searching through her handbag for that pen. She also pulls out a notebook and writes the name and address of the woman on the envelope. She lives in a town Claudia has visited, and to which she might very well return someday.

MONDAY

Dreaming

ONCE AGAIN, THE WOMAN who smokes only in public can barely pull herself out of bed. It makes no sense: the more she rests, the more tired she is.

She puts the coffee on, goes down to pick up the newspaper, comes back up without having so much as glanced at the headlines, puts the paper down on the edge of the table as she shuffles to the fridge to get her usual breakfast fare. She turns on the radio, a reflex. Goes to the bathroom, comes back, pours the coffee. And so on. A little later, as she dresses, she tries hard not to think of all the work waiting for her, promises herself to take the time to have some fun. But she immediately realizes that she has forgotten how. Dreams a moment of dropping everything and taking off. But she knows it's not time for that yet, wonders if there will ever be a right time. Worries she wouldn't recognize it if it did come. Or worse, would recognize it but let it pass, fail to seize the opportunity. Wonders if there really ever was a time in her life when everything was possible.

Carmen hops out of bed.

"You're awful excited! What's up, then?"

"Nothing. Don't know. I'm all wide awake this morning. Ouch!"

Carmen has stubbed her toe on the bedpost on her way to the bathroom.

"That'll teach you."

Terry hears the stream of urine in the bowl, likes even that of her. He falls half asleep waiting for her to come back. But Carmen takes her time.

"Well, are you coming back to bed or what?"

"I'm starting to have a belly. 'Bout time! Wasn't sure it was real. The whole thing, I mean. Being pregnant and all."

She climbs back into bed. Terry hugs her under the blankets, puts his hand on her belly.

"We ought to find a name for him."

"She's a girl, I think."

"Is that what you'd like, then?"

"Naw. Girl, boy, it's all the same to me. I hope it won't cry too much, though. Don't much care for babies who cry."

"You'll have to get used to it, won't you?"

"Don't I know it."

Neither speaks for a moment. Then:

"We ought to go into the bookstores today, read up on it — being pregnant, babies, giving birth, and all that. We could buy a book about it while we're at it."

"Would I have to be reading it too?"

"Wouldn't do any harm. I mean on account of you being the mother and all."

"Well, I suppose. You've got a point."

They lie in bed a little longer while the day gathers itself and begins. They wash up, and Carmen tries on the gift Terry gave her at the end of their day apart, a collection of seven panties, one for each day of the week. He liked that the days were written in French.

The man who'd shown no sign of reading had suddenly decided to go to Copenhagen instead of Israel. He'd never been to Denmark and had nothing in particular to do there, which were two perfectly good reasons to go.

He wanders awhile in the streets of the capital before going to Odense, just to see a bit more of the country. From time to time, his ear picks up a language he understands.

"You live in Denmark, but you don't live like the Danes."

The man who'd shown no sign of reading eavesdrops on a conversation between two white-collar workers at a nearby table.

"Is that a criticism?"

"I'm only saying that you're betraying your identity. Which is why one consumes your articles with a grain of salt."

The two men eat a moment in silence.

"Plus you were wrong about Maastricht, and you flip-flopped on the Euro."

The man to whom these remarks are addressed continues to chew on his food, takes a sip of wine.

"So you think I'm finished?"

His interlocutor considers this before replying.

"Depends. Maybe not. But watch out for those sudden U-turns. In your case, I'm not sure whether you ought to slow down or speed up. You know what they say about travesties . . ."

"And why not? That's what I'd like to know!"

"Don't know. Just doesn't suit you, is all."

Carmen pauses before completing her thought, hoping it won't be necessary to spell it out.

"Makes you look a bit of a poof."

She knew it wasn't a word to use lightly.

"A bit of a poof!"

Terry looks at himself again in the mirror, trying to see what Carmen sees. Not only does he not see it, but he really likes the coat.

"I really don't see what's poofish about it."

He buttons the jacket up to the neck, raises the collar, turns a little to the left, a little to the right. Carmen can see he likes the coat; she tries to soften the blow.

"Up like that, it's not so bad. Could be the colour. It's sort of shiny."

"Does it look cheap, then?"

Carmen thinks she's spotted a thread of doubt in Terry's mind, but she's careful not to reply too quickly. She doesn't want to give the impression of taking advantage of his hesitation.

"I suppose it does, in a way."

His hands in the pockets, Terry turns again in front of the mirror, a little to the left, a little to the right.

"I'm positive you can do better."

Now Terry looks uncertain. Carmen doesn't like to see him like this.

"Well, if you like it that much . . . I suppose it's not all that expensive."

Terry takes the coat off, puts it back on its hanger.

"I'm not so sure any more. I'll think on it awhile."

In the street, he adds: "You really think it makes me look a bit of a poof?"

Claudia gazes at the man who has returned, leaving a woman charmed and a boy calmed in his wake.

"What did you tell them? They really look much better."

"Not very much. It could be my voice. My mother used to say I had a voice of extinction."

Claudia is surprised by the expression. The man shrugs, laughs a little.

"I never knew if it was actually a compliment, though she did insist I call her often. She didn't mind how far away I lived, as long as I called so she could hear my voice."

Claudia listens to the man, trying to figure out what his mother meant. As a matter of fact, his voice does sound a bit as though it is being pitched into a deep well.

"Where did your mother live?"

"In the country near Dijon. She hardly left her little village."

The man has turned thoughtful. Claudia doesn't dare look at him.

Finally, he tells her: "You too must surely have some sort of power, a pole of attraction — how can I put it? — something indecipherable."

Claudia is nonplussed by his statement, which though he says it gently, nevertheless leaves her a little off balance.

"Maybe. I don't know."

The man places his hand on hers, looks at her with nothing but kindness.

"One day you'll know. And that day, if I have any luck, you'll remember me."

The man squeezes her hand gently before drawing back his arm. He looks at his watch.

"Well, I've got to go now."

He gets up, pays the bill, and returns to pick up the rest of his things. He offers Claudia a slight bow in lieu of a final farewell, or perhaps it's an *au revoir*. She can't decide.

Then he lets one or two seconds pass before concluding: "I wish you happiness."

Today Hans notices that the Band-Aids are on different fingers. The woman before him has also changed her hairdo; now it's a spectacular arrangement of curls and straight tresses.

"You would like to become no one, wouldn't you?"

Again, the woman does not wait for a reply.

"What's more, you believe you will become someone by becoming no one. It's a very old dilemma."

With that, the woman turns towards the Bay window. Hans perceives this as a turn away from any answer he might give, and he concludes once and for all that he is not here to talk about himself.

"Did you know that it was the fires more than the earthquakes that devastated San Francisco? The earthquakes certainly didn't help, but misfortunes travel in pairs. Nor does good fortune come alone, for that matter."

The woman turns back towards him. Hans notes that her swivel chair is well oiled.

"At this moment, you're not thinking about what I just said, are you?"

As a matter of fact, Hans is thinking that he must buy some oil for the squeaking armchair in his room.

"Well, that doesn't matter either. The important thing, really, is that many people come here with the ultimate hope of finding themselves, of making something of their lives. And every year, several hundred of them throw themselves off the Golden Gate Bridge. Speaking of which, have you ever walked across that bridge?"

As a matter of fact, no, Hans has never walked across.

And as if the accident hadn't been enough to shatter me completely, did the investigators have to botch their job as well? If they had done it properly, they would have realized that I was trying to close the glove compartment when that damned tug on the steering wheel pitched me into the way of the semi-trailer. Didn't they find me partly stretched out over the passenger seat, my fingers cut off in the open compartment? And if they had taken the trouble to check whether it was the radio or the tape deck that was on at the moment of impact, don't you think they might have asked themselves a few additional questions? After all, the music to which one chooses to die is not without importance.

Here, when I throw a tantrum, they barely look at me; they don't even give me the satisfaction of a what's-the-use. To them, it's simply laughable. I suspect that they wish I'd be reborn, reincarnated, and leave them in peace. In their eyes, my explanations don't hold water. As far as they're concerned, and here I choose my words carefully, to err is only human. I admit that, with time, such a vision tears gaps and punches holes in one's reasoning.

"You've experienced some small happiness recently. Perhaps yesterday or the day before. It's done something to you. I can see it."

It was true that in the light of his room on Telegraph Hill, Hans had discovered the grey-greenish tone of the ice at the foot of the mill in his jigsaw puzzle. The colour had struck him as exactly right and delightful, and he'd succeeded in assembling that entire section. The puzzle is advancing, and that too is a source of joy for Hans. He even hoped to see the Napa vineyard cowboy again, to tell him of the progress of his peculiar enterprise.

"Well? And how do you like your panties, then?"

Terry and Carmen are sitting at a terrace drinking coffee.

"Phew! I didn't think you were going to talk to me today."

"And why's that?"

"Don't know. You haven't said barely a word since morning, have you? I sure would like to know what's on your mind."

"Aw, not much. I'm just in my head, is all."

Terry's mood was all the more unsettling because the weather was truly gorgeous, a real spring day.

"Anyhow, I'd sure like to be in there as well. Inside your head, I mean."

Terry shrugs. "I suppose it's as good a place as any."

The therapist continues to chat to Hans about one thing or another until she wraps up the session. As she walks him to the door, she asks:

"What will you be doing tomorrow?"

Hans had not thought about it yet.

"Of all the days of the week, Tuesday is the one most

often chosen by suicides to throw themselves off the Golden Gate. It's a good day to go on the attack."

Hans freezes on the spot, but he can feel something like an air current sweep through his body.

The man who'd shown no sign of reading spent several days in Denmark, tuning in to conversations of which he understood at once everything and nothing, before travelling to Paris.

Sitting in a café, he thought he recognized the young man he'd met by the door to the washroom on the plane that brought him recently from Boston to London. The young woman seated beside him might very well be in the early stages of pregnancy, although it barely shows. The two young people are talking together, but they also look a little bored. The man cocks an ear.

"And tell me again, why was it we had to go through London instead of coming straight here?"

"It was cheaper for the open tickets, wasn't it?"

"Right. Aren't you the clever one to have unscrambled all that and got us all the way here."

The man who'd shown no sign of reading is no linguist, but he guesses the young people are speaking some sort of Caribbean dialect.

"And when are we off to Arles, then?"

"I'm not done working that out. Might be we'll start at Lyons. And what's your great hurry? I like it fine right here."

The man is no longer sure what dialect it is.

"Might be we shouldn't hold off too long. Anyway, we can come back here anytime, can't we? After the delta, I mean."

The two young people are silent for a bit.

Then: "A cigarette'd be nice right about now, wouldn't you say?"

"Oh, Lord, yes."

As was his habit after a session, Hans took his time walking home. He stopped to eat, allowed himself to be distracted here and there, did a bit of window shopping. Back in his room, he lay down on the bed to take a nap, legs crossed, hands behind his head. When he awoke, he lay a long time examining his room, the white walls, the transparent curtains on the windows, the majestic honey-coloured beams supporting the ceiling.

Still lying on his bed, he counts the small diamonds he's removed from the canvas pouch he carries around his neck. He has six left.

That evening, the woman who smokes only in public glances through the pages of Gorky to see what's in store for her there. She falls asleep rather quickly but wakes with a start. Without checking the time, she picks up the telephone.

"What's wrong?"

"I don't know. I feel terrified suddenly ."

"Where are you? At home?"

"Yes."

"I'm coming. Don't move."

A few minutes later, there's a knock on the door. The dark street is empty. The friend enjoys this sort of crisis.

"I brought my things. I'll sleep here."

They set up camp in the living room, sipping herbal tea.

"Now you see this can't go on! Do you enjoy suffering or what?"

The other woman says nothing.

"I mean, love is all right. But this guy is being *and* nothingness."

The other woman continues to say nothing.

"You ought to take a holiday, take a trip, see people."

The other woman shrugs as though none of that applies to her.

"I'm only saying it for your own good. You don't see yourself. You look like you're dying."

The other woman sighs, not entirely disagreeing.

"I don't know what you see in him. Okay, he's likeable. Charming, even. But he's a dreamer. You need someone less . . . more grounded."

The woman who smokes only in public still says nothing. Finally, she can think of only one thing.

"I know it's hard to understand, but I love him."

In a show of despair, the friend sinks into the sofa, although, in truth, she enjoys this sort of drama.

WEDNESDAY

Negotiation

THE DIAMOND MERCHANT silently examines one of the small stones, then another and another. Eventually, he examines all six. Hans, seated opposite, on the other side of a piece of furniture that is not quite a desk, watches him work.

The man consults a reference book with which he is clearly familiar, but he reveals neither what it is he's looking for nor whether he finds it, expressing neither surprise nor satisfaction. Hans, watching the silent occupations of the merchant, wonders if he was right to choose a jeweller at random.

At last the man stands.

"Do you mind?"

He flattens the canvas bag on his palm and lays the six small precious stones on top, moves into the next room, still without saying anything. Hans trusts him. He has a feeling the diamond merchant is a modest man.

The merchant reappears, regains his position behind the sort of desk. He spreads the diamond bag carefully over the surface and sits down. Once seated, he places his elbows on the not-quite desk, pressing his hands together, as though in prayer but somewhat more loosely, without the fervour of prayer. He exhales in short bursts on the tips of his fingers, which touch the centre of his lips.

Ever since she mailed it, Claudia can't stop thinking about the letter the man who'd shown no sign of reading entrusted to her.

"You look worried. Something wrong?"

"I guess I can't wait to go home. I'm not doing much of anything here."

Claudia knows she can say this sort of thing to her mother without offending her.

"Too bad we didn't have more free time, but your father is so busy."

"He looks tired."

The mother pauses a moment before replying.

"I hurt him badly recently."

This confession surprises Claudia.

"I was intending to tell you the whole story, but I haven't had the nerve. Now time is pressuring me."

The mother pauses again, finds the courage to continue.

"I'm not sure that I still love him."

Another pause.

"To tell the truth, I think I've tried my best. But I can't go on any more. It's beyond me."

The mother pauses once more, then realizes there's nothing more to say.

"It's awful, I know."

And though she recognizes that this is an ideal moment to embrace her daughter, to reassure her, the mother can't quite bring herself to do it. She fears the worst. She fears that love no longer reassures at all.

The diamond merchant's slow pace is beginning to intrigue Hans. The man leafs through his reference book again, goes over a calculation, turns his gaze once more upon the six small diamonds. Hans thinks maybe he should have thrown the diamonds off the bridge yesterday. Because he did indeed walk across the Golden Gate on a Tuesday. He even stopped awhile along the railing, and he admired the gentle roiling of the sea at the bay's entrance.

"They're perfect. Exquisite, even. I can't pay you what they're worth, but I would very much like to have them. For a jeweller friend of mine. He's terribly talented, but to tell the truth, it's a talent he can't afford. Life is strange, isn't it?"

With this question, which is really an affirmation, the diamond merchant extends his arm almost lazily to reach a ring binder on the shelf, then brings it down, places it before Hans, and begins to turn the pages. It contains a series of photographs of original works of jewellery combining an infinite variety of metals and stones, the curves and lines of which create highly uncommon effects, as though the stones were floating or suspended in air.

"Jewellery looks larger in photos. This one, for example, is hardly bigger than a dime."

Having pointed out the jewel in question, the diamond merchant continues to turn the pages of the binder.

"He's an odd bird, really. He lives — I should say survives — in a small village in northern Italy. But at heart, he's a vagabond."

The man extends a hand, picks up a postcard, rereads it in silence, smiles at something, places the card on the not-quite desk.

"Avignon."

Hans turns the pages of the binder himself.

"Me, I'm a businessman. But I admire him because he couldn't care less about business."

The man interrupts Hans's mechanical page-turning and leafs back to a page at the end of the binder.

"He gave this piece to a young girl who one day offered to carry an old woman's groceries up the steep hills of her village to her house. Just like that. Gave it away. He could have sold it for three or four thousand dollars."

Staring at the piece in question, Hans imagines first the old lady, then the young girl, then the steep hills of the village. He goes back to those pages of the binder he hasn't yet examined.

"Sometimes he sells one. He has no choice. From time to time, I provide him with some material. You see, he's a genius."

Terry enters the *boulangerie.* He's beginning to feel at home here. They greet him like an old customer.

"Baguette and chocolatine for *monsieur?*"

The large dolled-up woman has already begun to prepare the order. There's little danger of her making a mistake, since Terry has been buying exactly the same thing every morning for a week now.

As he leaves the bakery, Terry decides to stop for a quick coffee. He knows that Carmen is sleeping comfortably and decides she will appreciate the few additional minutes.

Standing at the counter, Terry feels someone tap him on the shoulder. He turns to see a face that is not entirely unfamiliar, but that he can't quite place.

"This is the third time our paths have crossed. Your girlfriend, or wife, was throwing up in the washroom on the airplane. She seems to be feeling better."

"Yes. She's preggers."

"Yes, I know."

Now Terry remembers the man.

"A few days ago, I saw the two of you sitting at a terrace not far from here. I gather you live nearby? I'm staying close by as well."

The man who'd shown no sign of reading orders a coffee. Terry finds a thread to continue the conversation.

"You're travelling too, then?"

"Yes. Well . . . something like that."

Claudia is packing her bags in her room in her parents' small apartment. Though she doesn't feel completely overwhelmed, she realizes that things are no longer as they were. Which is why she concentrates on the immediate present, on one thing at a time. Her mother is seated on the bed.

"I thought I might go back to the States. I'd like to be near you."

Claudia hears this but says nothing. She's not against the idea; on the other hand, she's not about to jump for joy.

"I could find a job. We might even live together."

Again, Claudia says nothing.

"But not necessarily. You're a big girl. I'd understand if you didn't feel the need."

Claudia still doesn't know what to say, so she says nothing.

"Your father will stay here, I think. He doesn't have the strength to do anything else for the moment."

Claudia pauses a moment, bent over an open drawer.

"And where were you?"

"I know. I wasn't thinking to be gone so long, but then I ran into that man and we got to yapping."

Terry tells Carmen about the man who recognized him in the café.

"And that would be tonight?"

"I'm telling you, the fellow's got a nice way about him."

While Carmen considers the proposal, Terry adds: "We've nothing to lose."

"Don't know. It's a bit weird, don't you think?"

"Not all that much. I mean, it's only for supper. And we're in Paris now, aren't we? It's not like we're in some backwoods place."

"Not so sure I can wait until eight o'clock to eat. You know how it is."

"Well, he says he's going there for supper anyhow, so we've only to join him if we feel like it."

"Will he be paying, then?"

"Sounded that way."

Carmen looks about ready to accept.

"Well, we ought to go by the restaurant during the day, just to make sure it's not some dive."

The woman who smokes only in public is not sure how it happened, but she no longer feels helpless. She's even confident that things will work out. And yet, she's decided nothing, made no plan. She's simply continuing to live.

"You've seen your doctor?"

"No. Why?"

"You look better. I thought perhaps you'd followed my advice."

"No. I just feel better, that's all."

The friend who'd tried so hard to lift the spirits of the woman who smokes only in public remains sceptical.

"I accept. That's all."

"You accept."

"That's right. I accept."

"But what exactly do you accept?"

"Everything."

"Everything."

"Yes. Everything."

The friend finds the woman facing her evasive, or simplistic.

"You accept to forget?"

"Not in the least!"

The friend is slightly uncomfortable. She gazes out the café window, sees the people hurrying, hopes to reground the conversation by saying something banal.

"You're not smoking today?"

"Oh, right. I almost forgot."

The friend, now completely bewildered, can only laugh.

"That's it. I've stepped through the looking glass."

Hans accepted the diamond merchant's offer and went home. Lying on his bed, he thinks again about his walk across the bridge. He saw no one throw themself off, but at one point, he thought another pedestrian was looking at him strangely. Perhaps the man thought that he, Hans, would take the plunge. Something he considered, of course.

Hans gets up, approaches the puzzle. His eye falls on a piece that he has been looking for these past few days. He snaps the piece into place, finds another and another; the pieces come forward themselves, fall into place. The jigsaw puzzle has become a mere game, something has moved.

The days pass; a kind of lethargy has set in. Life on earth seems farther and farther away, vaporous. I move more easily among the precise suicides. I seem to fit here among them after all. I'm even getting used to the idea that compared with some of you, I really did choose to die; that in relation to some of you, there was no other choice. Suicide may not be as exact a gesture as I originally thought. I thought I wanted to live. Even here, I continued to cling to the idea of living. But with time, such convictions diminish. Both reality and one's point of view change. Or rather, they come together.

I would like to offer you loftier, more reassuring thoughts. I would like to comfort you in your truths. But the hours grow calm here, increasingly calm. I think I am really dying.

Claudia snaps one of her suitcases shut.

"It's not so bad, really."

Her mother hears but does not react. She has ceased waiting for her daughter to speak.

"Joy is still possible. We only have to know how to

find it. Let's go to the restaurant, all three of us. I'll finish packing tomorrow before leaving."

Claudia does not wait for her mother's reply before calling her father, who appears in the doorway.

"Are you coming to the restaurant with us?"

The father looks first at the mother, then at the daughter. He's not sure he understands.

"And put on your good shirt. Afterwards, maybe we'll go dancing."

The father looks again at the mother and the daughter, shrugs, and submits without further entreaties.

Hans's skill with the puzzle that afternoon was so great that he almost forgot his appointment.

"You have been freed, relieved of something. Something has fallen away from you like a crust. Things can now come through to you, reach you. The obstruction is gone. And something more. You've become a pole, a focus of attention. Your jigsaw puzzle is progressing now, isn't it? The pieces just pop up before your eyes, don't they?"

Once again, the woman with the chewed-up fingers does not wait for a reply. She swivels in her chair, turns towards the Bay window.

"Some afflictions dissipate of themselves. And in resolving themselves, they teach us things. Our bodies register all this. Our bodies know everything. Everything."

The woman turns back to Hans.

"You've no further need to come here. You're free. You will always make the right choices."

When it comes time to pay, the woman again refuses Hans's money.

"No. You still need it. One day, very soon, when it's really of no use to you, you'll have no difficulty finding someone to give it to. Go. Be happy."

That evening, engrossed in his puzzle, which takes shape before his eyes, Hans is convinced that he began to make the right choices the day he decided to sell all his belongings and take to the road.

Terry and Carmen do their best to chat with the man who'd shown no sign of reading. The restaurant is packed, the decor charming, the wine exquisite.

"The Rhone delta?"

"Yup. We're thinking we ought to begin from Lyons."

"When?"

"Depends. We're in no rush. And what about you? Where is it you're going, then?"

Carmen is amused. Terry looks so serious. As though he is trying to be a real grown-up. She feels like taking the girl's part.

"I was supposed to go to Israel, but I don't feel like it any more. That's how I travel, without any particular goal. It can sometimes be a bit boring, but I enjoy thinking through it afterwards, when it's over."

"And where is it you're from?"

The waiter arrives with the main course before the man can reply. Terry and Carmen are impressed by the lovely arrangement of the food on the plates. The question, momentarily forgotten, is raised again later.

"My things are in Baltimore. With a woman I love."

Whatever idea Terry had of Baltimore, it is severely shaken at that moment. Carmen, for her part, struggles to conciliate the practices of roaming and love. A few moments of silence pass before the next question.

"What is it you do in your travels?"

The man notes the somewhat baroque formulation.

"I'm a painter, or ex-painter. I don't know any more."

"Really?"

Terry and Carmen would have liked the man to elaborate, but nothing follows. Terry therefore once again takes up the harness.

"I suppose it must be nice to travel that way. With all there is to see, I mean."

The man nods his head a bit, to say yes in a way, but mostly no. Then he states flatly: "I needed to be doing nothing special."

Terry and Carmen acquiesce, instantly grasping the concept.

"I admire your wish to see the Rhone delta. It's been a long time since I had a longing like that, a real, concrete desire. I'm a little odd that way."

Terry and Carmen feel a great sympathy for the man, whom they don't find all that odd. They exchange a glance. Carmen feels joyful; she nods discreet encouragement to Terry to go on.

"Would you like to come along with us, then? If you've nothing else to do . . ."

The man thanks them for the invitation, saying he can't accept. But no sooner are the words out of his mouth than he is overcome by a sudden impulse.

"Actually, yes. I'd like that. I'd love to come."

In the restaurant, Claudia's heart is as light as a feather. She feels as though she has gone, without the slightest confusion, from being a young girl to becoming a young woman. It happened smoothly, in a matter of weeks, maybe even days. She knows now that she needs her own secrets, and that's why she wasn't able to tell her parents everything. What would they have understood of the wanderings of the man who'd shown no sign of reading? She preferred not to know. From now on, she needs to maintain her own point of view. This evening, dancing in her father's arms, Claudia, not wishing to precipitate anything, tries very hard to continue to be the young girl she was. Walking towards the table, where her mother sits watching them return from the dance floor, she's far from sure she has succeeded.

SATURDAY

Evaluation

"DOES HE SEEM a bit cuckoo to you?"

"Not really. Seems nice to me. You'd think he was one of us."

"That's true. I know exactly what you mean. He doesn't yap on and on about everything and anything."

The man who'd shown no sign of reading has left the compartment to get some coffee.

"How long do you suppose he'll stick around with us, then?"

Terry shrugs. "His bag's not very big, is it?"

"I like his coat. That's the sort you ought to have."

Terry looks at the coat hanging on a hook.

"Looks long to me."

Carmen grabs a tail between her fingers, rubs the cloth lightly. She gets up and reads the label inside the collar.

"Just what I was thinking. Cashmere."

Carmen sits back down, takes Terry's hand in hers, and inhales a deep, happy breath as she watches the scenery flow by.

"It's exciting, though, wouldn't you say?"

Hans whistles softly as he takes his time fitting the final bits into the puzzle. Fewer than two dozen pieces lie close at hand. They are coloured blue, grey, and green, and they make up the sky in the top right-hand corner of the image. Since his last appointment with the woman with the chewed-up cuticles, he has devoted virtually all of his waking time to the puzzle. He no longer knows if he is completing it for the sake of pleasure or simply to be done with it. He feels that he has already moved on to something else. The time spent fitting all the pieces together has nevertheless allowed him to think, to let his mind wander. He's watched hundreds of possibilities flare up brightly, only to let them drift off to their separate fates. One of these, however, has continually resurfaced, and Hans knows very well that it is in this direction that he must act.

Claudia finishes emptying her suitcases. She put away most of her things the day after she got back, but she didn't have the heart to eliminate these last traces of her trip.

"Here, it's yours. Humour is almost as important as love. I would say the two often go hand in hand."

Again the pope-rabbi, and again seated next to her! Claudia had thought she was dreaming.

In the end, because it was easier that way, she had accepted the small book of jokes on the theme of God that the pope-rabbi offered her. He'd read a few pages, smiling, and later burst out laughing. That's when he turned to Claudia to tell her the joke. Claudia, unsure whether she got it, laughed out of politeness, but without really giving the impression that she'd understood.

Then, in a sudden generous impulse, the pope-rabbi had offered her the book.

Someone's at the door. Hans recognizes the knock of his Spanish-speaking neighbour, the one who's always asking to borrow matches. The first time he came, Hans gave him the only matches he had. The second time, a few days later, Hans told him he had none and the fellow had run off in embarrassment, only to return with a packet a few minutes later. Possibly he thought that no one could manage without matches. Through this relationship based on matches, the neighbour and Hans saw each other several times a week. It had become a game, an easy and innocent way to express their friendship, as a result of which Hans had developed the habit of maintaining a provision of matches.

Hans opens the door, steps over to a small cupboard to pick up a book of matches, returns to the half-open door. The neighbour points to the jigsaw puzzle, which needs only four or five pieces to be complete. Hans invites him to take a closer look. The young Hispanophone admires the work, passes a hand over the surface, and, indicating the few loose pieces, invites Hans to complete the puzzle in his presence. Hans does not react. The neighbour insists. Hans resists, shakes his head, and motions no with his hands. The neighbour eyes Hans for a moment, pretends to guess what he is up to, and finally laughs; tapping Hans on the shoulder in agreement, he takes the matches and goes. Alone again, Hans wonders what his neighbour could possibly have concluded.

The man who'd shown no sign of reading is seated with a cup of coffee in his hand.

"So what's Moncton like?"

Terry and Carmen look at each other. Each can see in the other's face the lack of ready-made descriptions. Finally, Terry laughs.

"It's a fine place to look at when it snows. In the evenings."

The man sitting opposite them traces a quick sketch in his mind.

"Lots of cities are beautiful if one doesn't dwell on the details."

Terry and Carmen think some more.

"There's some streets have big houses and big trees."

"At Christmastime, with the decorations and all, that helps."

"Are the houses made of wood or stone?"

"Folks would say they're wood, I suppose. We don't really think of them that way. They're just . . . houses, is all."

Terry and Carmen try to think of something else to say,

embarrassed at not being able to come up with much. Then Terry finds something he considers significant.

"There's a whole lot of artists, though. Folks who paint, I mean."

"Is that right?"

"They say the place's special for that. . . . Not that I know much about it."

"Special how?"

Terry and Carmen exchange another consultative gaze. Carmen tries her luck.

"I suppose it's the colours. You might say they're . . . well, big."

"Big?"

"Yeah. Big. Thick."

Terry feels there's more to it.

"Not only that, mind you. There's a whole lot. Artists, I mean. For a such a wee place."

Carmen risks something more.

"Can't say they're all pretty, though."

Terry is intrigued.

"And which of them is it you're thinking of, then?"

"Well, the one over at the library, when you're coming down the staircase."

"Mmm . . ."

The memory of that particular painting propels Terry and Carmen into a moment of deathly silence, but they eventually resurface.

"There's one of them, Yvon Gallant, who can paint anything."

"That's the truth. That fellow's unbelievable. Not that

it's all perfect to begin with, but in the end, you can't help liking it."

"There's another, Paul Bourque. You might say, he mixes things around. Won't sell his stuff, though. Doesn't want to. Which is why everyone wants to buy them. Pretty sharp, if you ask me."

"And then there's Roméo Savoie."

"Hermé."

"There's a fellow does everything — writes, paints, makes movies, writes plays. Can't think of anything he doesn't do."

"Those are just the ones best known. There's a whole lot more."

"Raymond Martin."

"Raymond Martin, Nancy Morin, Guy Duguay — well, he's dead."

"There was Denise Daigle too."

"Yup. Denise."

"Francis Coutellier . . . Luc Charette . . ."

"Dyane Léger . . . And what's the name of that other one, works next to Yvon in the other room?"

"Lionel Cormier."

"And what about Alexandria?"

"Alexandria Eaton. English, that one. But she's okay, just the same."

"Jacques Arsenault."

"Really, there's a whole bunch of them."

"Gilles LeBlanc's not too shabby neither."

"There's always an opening going on somewhere, with wine and bits of food to eat as well. Anyone can go."

"The more business-minded ones often have the smoked salmon."

"Lots of them don't have loads of money, but they get by just the same."

The spontaneous enumeration amuses the man who'd shown no sign of reading.

"Have you bought paintings?"

"Yvon Gallant gave us one. A small one. That time we drove him to Halifax to see an exhibition. He doesn't drive himself."

"I'd like us to have one of Dyane Léger's for our boy's room. Or girl. We don't know which yet."

"There's Francis Coutellier as well. His boats are pretty nice too."

"You see, there again, it's the colour."

"There's George Blanchette as well."

"For the kid's room?"

"Well, no. I mean, just to have."

Hans inserts the last piece of the puzzle without ceremony. He hadn't noticed, before fitting it in, that the shades on this last piece seem to represent a castle or a church. He bends down, examines it more closely. He can't decide if it's a detail intended by the artist or an effect resulting from the angle of the brush on the canvas.

Hans now begins to study the painting in search of other details that may have escaped him. He finds himself enjoying again those elements he had previously admired, and he discovers a few others that also please him. Later, he will continue to glance at the work from a distance while, sitting cross-legged on his bed, he has a bite to eat.

Claudia is cleaning up her desk, putting books and notebooks away, stacking those she will have to open before starting her courses again. She checks her watch, makes a phone call but does not leave a message on the answering machine. She washes up, redials the earlier number. Still no one. She dresses and goes out anyway.

The sun is shining and a warm wind is blowing on the avenue. Claudia lingers in front of a few shop windows, goes into a record store, buys something, comes out, walks some more, goes into a café, hails a waiter, sits, pulls a magazine out of her bag while she waits to be served.

"You're a musician?"

"No, not at all."

"Strange. I could have sworn."

Claudia found it odd that during the return trip, the pope-rabbi had asked her the same question as had the man who'd shown no sign of reading. She had no idea what it was in her appearance or attitude that would lead people to think she was a musician.

"You're the second person to ask me that recently."

"Your neck, your shoulders give that impression. Mainly your neck, I think. It seems as though music would pass through there. It's a fine passage."

With that, the pope-rabbi had fallen silent. Even though he maintained a kind of joviality in spite of everything, Claudia sensed he'd somehow changed in the past two weeks.

"My mother doesn't love my father any more. She's going to leave him. She's thinking of coming to America."

"It's normal that she'd want to be closer to you. How about your father?"

"He's sad, a little down."

"He'll get over it, although . . ."

Claudia waited a moment for the pope-rabbi to complete the sentence, but the end did not come.

The more time passes, the less I'm certain of what happened that day. I'm no longer sure what I was thinking when I saw that truck coming from the opposite direction. I remember it was a nice day, but something like an undertow seemed to be pulling down on the idyllic scene. I felt a need to spread myself thin over the surface of things, as though I were repulsed by my need to hold fast. But hold fast to what? In the name of what? I believe I might have thought about giving the wheel that fatal twist, but I also believe I was afraid I'd end up surviving and paralyzed. I wanted to clear my head, put some music on. I looked for Barencourt's *Orphaned Notes*. The cassette wasn't in its usual place. The truck was bearing down.

If I had my life to live over again, although . . .

"Well, weren't you the brainy-sounding one, then."

"I had to think up something to say, didn't I? I never thought I knew so many artists."

Carmen had been amused by Terry's observations on Acadian art.

"No, truly. It sounded swell. Sometimes you really impress me."

The man who'd shown no sign of reading returns from the washroom, sits, watches the countryside file past.

"It's my first time in Lyons."

They had decided to rent a car in Lyons and follow the river down to the Mediterranean. No one could say how long it would take. Certainly days, perhaps weeks.

Hans is busy photocopying the cover of the jigsaw puzzle's box. It takes him several tries before he's satisfied that he's captured the colours as accurately as possible and the dimensions he wants. He pays the clerk, walks a few blocks, enters a supermarket, buys a box of clear plastic bags, the strong ones used for storing frozen foods.

Back in his room, Hans breaks the puzzle apart and pours the pieces into one of the bags. He is glad he bought the large size. He presses the zip-lock — he enjoys that sensation — then slips the bag, zip-lock end first, into a second identical bag, a precaution in case the first bag breaks open, allowing some pieces to escape. Satisfied with the result, and with the malleability of the package — the original puzzle box would have taken up too much room — he now cuts off the white edges of the best of the photocopies of the painting, slips it between the two layers of plastic, and seals the second bag. He takes a few moments to handle the reinforced package, which produces a pleasing sound. Finally, he tidies up and takes his suitcase out of the cupboard. He places the puzzle in the bottom and the rest of his things on top. In no time at all, though he has not hurried, his packing is done. Hans scribbles a few words on a piece of paper, which he leaves, along with some bills, on the table now cleared of the puzzle. He picks up his things, exits and locks the door of the room, deposits the key in a place previously designated by the owner — you can't be too careful — and leaves the house.

"Some people toss their own bottle in the ocean. They send it out, and then one day it comes back to them. And it becomes their salvation."

At first, Claudia didn't understand what the pope-rabbi meant, especially since his pronouncement seemed to rise up like a pyramid in the midst of silence. She took the time to think before replying.

"You mean like Little Thumb in the fairy tale?"

"Yes, a little. But it's less thought out, much more innocent. Little Thumb knew what he was doing, didn't he?"

"Yes, I think so."

The pope-rabbi thought awhile.

"No, I wouldn't say that people do it on purpose, or

that they even hold out much hope. But they do have some sort of idea in mind."

The pope-rabbi didn't seem to expect any reply.

"The earth spins on its axis; we tend to forget that. Perhaps it too ends up catching up to itself, meeting up with itself."

Claudia certainly had nothing to add to that.

"The fact that I meet you again in this plane, for example. What pure chance, don't you think? But then, what is chance?"

Coming out of the Lyons train station exit, Carmen pauses in front of the makeshift stand of a bearded man selling jewellery.

"They sure are pretty."

"Must be awful expensive."

Carmen points to one of the items.

"Look. That one's like a delta. Wouldn't that make a fine souvenir?"

Terry joins Carmen in admiring the quasi-triangular brooch with its five small, brilliant stones. Arriving on the scene, the man who'd shown no sign of reading also looks at the modest yet surprising display.

"These jewels are original, aren't they?"

Terry asks the bearded man how much he wants for the brooch Carmen likes and calculates the price in dollars.

"Two hundred and fifty. That's a bit steep."

"Steep is right!"

The man who'd shown no sign of reading intervenes.

"If you'll allow me, I'd like to buy it for you. As a kind of general gift, for the trip, for the baby . . ."

Carmen looks at Terry. Terry looks at the man.

"You've really no cause to be giving us a gift. You're paying for plenty of things as it is."

"But it would be my pleasure."

The bearded man undoes the pin from the cloth of the display and shows how pretty it looks on Carmen's coat.

"It suits you beautifully. Come on, I insist!"

The man who'd shown no sign of reading takes out his wallet to pay the peddler. He selects an additional pin, this one set with only one stone but skilfully displayed.

"And this one as well."

"That one's two thousand francs."

The man who'd shown no sign of reading makes a rapid calculation and looks squarely at the peddler, who appears to find the situation very amusing.

"For the young lady, one thousand. For you, two thousand. . . . But they're worth far more."

Again, the man who'd shown no sign of reading looks the bearded man in the eye, to see if he's telling the truth. He has the feeling that he is.

A young man joins Claudia in the café.

"I thought I'd find you here."

He takes his coat off and sits down.

"You bought a record, I see."

Claudia passes him the small bag. The young man opens it, looks at the contents.

"You know it?"

"No. It looked good."

Claudia shrugs, adds in a cheerful voice: "I felt like trying."

SUNDAY

Rest

THE WOMAN WHO smokes only in public slowly paces the length of the airport arrivals lounge. She got here very early, having no desire to do anything else. She thinks again about the phone call that came a few days ago.

"Gorky? Oh . . ."

A brief silence followed, then:

"But tell me, do people really want to read Gorky again?"

In this almost ordinary question she had recognized the candour and tender astonishment that this man experienced daily as he went about the activity — strange activity for him — of living, an occupation that he nonetheless assumed with a degree of constancy.

"Where are you?"

"In France. A little south of Lyons."

The woman sensed he was telling the truth, though she had not expected such a frank reply.

For a moment, neither one could think what to say.

"Gorky. Well, well . . ."

Then she guessed.

"You're coming home?"

"Yes. I'm coming home."

It's been days since I thought of you, my son, my wife — why do I persist in calling you that? — days since I thought of all of you on earth. I'm constantly drifting farther away, changing. Since I passed beyond the stage of light, I have felt myself dilating more and more, spreading more and more into the empty, moving heart of matter.

At times, though these sightings are increasingly rare, bits and pieces of your existence briefly reflect on my clouded consciousness. But I find it more and more difficult to answer you. I seem to have lost that ability somehow. I no longer have any position whatsoever. I am the inner lining of old thoughts. I can't any more. I simply can't. I just am.

"I can't believe they're real diamonds. Seems to me, makes no sense."

"I know. It's hard to believe."

Carmen is sitting on the bed in their tiny room in Arles, looking at the brooch she holds between her fingers.

"Well, it's a bit nerve-racking, isn't it? I mean, what if we lost it?"

Terry looks out the window to think better. He realizes that it's the first time he's sensed Carmen so perturbed.

"Well, we can't stop living, can we, on account of some bauble?"

"I know, but just think about it! Now we've got the thing, if we were to lose it . . ."

"They're only diamonds. I mean, it's not like they're

alive. They're rocks. Dead things. It's not as if you were to lose the baby."

"For heaven's sake! Why'd you go and say that!"

Terry comes over to sit beside Carmen on the bed, puts his hand on her belly.

"All I'm saying is, this is the important thing. Not those diamonds."

Carmen is quiet, allows herself to be consoled.

Then: "I never for one second thought we could lose the baby."

"Fine. So don't go scaring yourself with that now."

"Okay. Just don't go saying that again, ever."

They lie back on the bed a moment, lost in thought.

"What do you want to do now? We ought to go out for a walk, put some fresh air in our heads."

Carmen's reply is slow in coming.

"Odd. It's kind of like the trip's not the same any more all of a sudden."

Terry understands what she means, tries to figure out what's changed.

Carmen adds: "He left in an awful hurry, wouldn't you say?"

"That's how it is sometimes. When you gotta go, you gotta go."

"I suppose so."

As he steps off the bus in Baltimore, Hans feels with absolute certainty that he has one thing to do: begin his life again. All those days crossing the United States from west to east, he hadn't felt it this clearly. On the road, as though he was hampered by too much ballast, by the weight of possessions, he had mainly concentrated on ridding himself of his money, giving it casually to whoever seemed to feel they needed it. He could not bear the head start the money gave him. He did not want a head start, not over himself or over others. He wanted to live at point zero, always. To occupy himself with living, and no more. Sleeping in rudimentary shelters, finding every day something to eat in exchange for some service or menial labour, but without further engagement. Without compromising himself. And without fear of losing his balance. Allowing each day to give birth to its own particular equilibrium or necessary folly.

As Hans steps off the bus, therefore, the day, and life in general, looks good to him: he slept a little badly; his jacket is wrinkled, having served as a pillow on the journey; and there's a stain above the knee of one of his pant legs. Only his expensive leather suitcase makes him slightly uncomfortable. He looks over the scene briefly, selects a street that seems promising, sets out with the goal of meeting someone who will take his bag in exchange for a canvas sac he can carry on his shoulder.

Terry can see that Carmen has done her very best, although without quite managing to regain her good mood. She agreed to tag along with Terry into town, but she seems to have lost her drive, her usual curiosity.

"You really want to go to the Museum of Pagan Art?"

"Seems to me it'd be something to see. And we'd have been to at least one museum. Might look better — once we got back, I mean — if we did."

Carmen stirs her espresso slowly. She prefers it sweet.

"It's as though I've lost interest in the whole trip. I kinda feel like a delta myself."

"I can see that, on account of the way the baby's going to come out from between your legs wide open."

Carmen had not thought of it quite that way, but Terry's description adds weight to her feeling.

"Well, there's that as well, I suppose. I was thinking more on account of we'll be three from now on. I guess I'm seeing myself more like a triangle now."

Terry says nothing, allows Carmen the time to unravel her feelings.

"Don't know what's the matter with me! It's like I don't understand the trip any more."

"Could be you're just tired. After all, you're pregnant. That must do something to a person."

"Could be."

Suddenly, Carmen begins to sob. Terry has never seen her cry. He brings his chair closer, wraps his arms around her, trying to console her.

"That's okay, then. Don't you worry one bit. I'm here with you, aren't I?"

Carmen sobs even harder. She knows she's in public, but she can't help it.

"I swear, I don't know myself any more."

Terry squeezes her shoulders tight, lets her cry a bit longer before speaking.

"Could be you're bored, is all."

Carmen doesn't quite know what she feels, but she certainly hadn't thought of that. Her crying begins to abate.

"Are you bored, then?"

Terry realizes, to his amazement, that he's not bored one bit, but he decides it's best to lie a little.

"Sometimes."

Claudia chose the train rather than the bus to get from Baltimore to Philadelphia. When the time had come to choose a college to complete her studies, she'd picked Philadelphia over Washington without really knowing why, but she's never regretted her decision. As for the train, she knows only that she likes the gentle rocking, the chief conductor doing his rounds, giving the voyage an official stamp. At the station in Baltimore, she checks the departure time to return the same day, then she sets out into the city, in search of the neighbourhood of the woman to whom was addressed the envelope she had mailed for the man who'd shown no sign of reading.

Terry and Carmen are back in their room. They're stretched out on the bed. Terry is reading with Carmen huddled up against him. Her eyes are shut, but she's not sleeping.

"Funny how I feel. Can't say as I understand it, but there's a whole lot of stuff happening just now."

"Inside you, you mean?"

"Inside me and not inside me. I'm telling you, I can't understand it."

"Could be that's what travelling does."

"Could be. It's awful weird, anyway."

"It's Sunday too."

"And what might that have to do with it, pray tell?"

"Well, Sunday's the only day that's not like the others, isn't it?"

"On account of Mass?"

"Sunday Mass, Sunday mess. Sunday's just like that, is all. Boring and mixed up, like. Always been like that for me. When I was a kid, Sundays I was all in pieces. I just wanted Monday to hurry up and come. Things could only get better."

"And did they? Get better, I mean?"

Again Terry decides it's best to lie a little.

"Always."

The woman who smokes only in public is driving full speed on the highway. The man who'd shown no sign of reading is sitting next to her.

"You got my note from Israel?"

"Yes. Thanks. It was a nice thought."

The woman hesitates before asking the question on her mind.

"Did you really go there?"

The man, on the other hand, does not hesitate at all.

"No. It was too much."

"Too much?"

"Yes, too much. I was afraid that I wouldn't be able to breathe, that I'd collapse from within."

"You, afraid?"

"Yes. Me. Afraid."

In the face of this frank admission, the woman reaches out, puts her hand on the man's arm, squeezes a bit.

"Do you think you'll want to paint again?"

"I don't know. Maybe. I know only that I don't want to live without you any more."

Hans is walking down the sun-drenched avenue, his hands in his pockets, the canvas bag over his shoulder and swinging gently against his back. He found exactly the sort of bag he was looking for, one of those seabags with a wide strap and an opening that pulls shut, thanks to a rope that laces through a series of eyelets.

As he walks along, he is trying to decide whether to destroy all his identification papers. He weighs the pros and cons, evaluating the degree of satisfaction such a gesture would afford him. He thinks of the woman with the chewed-up fingers, realizes that she was right, that he does indeed aspire to become someone by becoming nobody. He can also hear her telling him that he will always make the right choices. As a result, Hans feels no need to hurry his decision. He will decide in good time. He has a more pressing desire to rid himself of the jigsaw puzzle, which he is still carrying in his bag. Because it seems to him to be an object of some interest, he does not want to simply throw it away.

In the bed in the small room in Arles, Carmen is sleeping against Terry, who puts his book down to watch her. He hopes she will awaken free of the worry and confusion that inhabited her at the beginning of the day. He also remembers the conversation he had alone with the man who'd shown no sign of reading.

"Watching the two of you, it seems so obvious, so simple."

Terry, sensing the time had come, ventured to adopt a more personal tone.

"Love, you mean?"

"We call it that, but . . ."

Terry waited for the conclusion, but realizing that nothing would follow, he made another stab at it.

"It's true it's more than meets the eye. And anyway, I mean, after all, what else is there?"

"I've found nothing else."

"Is that what you were looking for, then? Some other thing?"

"Some other thing, or someone else but me, beyond me. I found only me."

But immediately the man seemed to amend his conclusion.

"No, not quite. Beyond me, I found what was there before me. Darkness and wind."

Terry found this description somewhat depressing, but the man seemed rather happy.

"That's it. Exactly. Now I understand. I was trying to find how to retain the light. But we don't have to retain it; it appears all on its own. Yes, that's it. It makes itself. Like now."

And the man became exceedingly cheerful, talking about one thing and another, until finally: "Have you been to Vent Couvert?"

"No, but my dad worked there a spell when I was a boy."

"Did he?"

"Not long, mind you. He missed my mum too much."

"She didn't want to go along?"

"No. Don't know why not. Never really understood the whys and wherefores of that story."

Claudia asked the taxi driver to drop her off a few blocks before the street she was looking for. She wanted to cross the neighbourhood on foot, since the weather was fine and she had plenty of time to spare. Now she finds herself across the street from the house of the woman to whom the man who'd shown no sign of reading had addressed his letter. The mid-sized house includes elements of modern design. Nevertheless, it blends nicely with the neighbourhood, which, though not entirely chic, is clean and comfortable.

From her position in the entrance of a small apartment building, Claudia is content to watch the quiet comings and goings of her surroundings. She notices that though some people greet each other, not everyone seems to know everyone else. Some passersby look at her, others not at all. She stands there for close to a quarter of an hour without spotting any movement around the house opposite. There's no car in the yard, and the garage door is closed. She knows very well that she will not go across and knock on the door. She never had the slightest intention of doing any such thing. She simply wanted to see the house, the place, to somehow prolong the story or imagine new aspects of it. Now that it's done, she's thinking of leaving, of walking a little more in the streets and taking her train back to Philadelphia.

Claudia is about to set out when a car enters the lane of the house. Her heart leaps. A woman gets out from the driver's side, and then, from the other side, emerges the man who'd shown no sign of reading. Claudia retreats into the entrance of the building, not wishing to be seen. The woman and the man step to the rear of the car; the woman opens the trunk, the man removes two suitcases. Claudia recognizes one of these. The woman goes towards the door of the house while the man closes the trunk and picks up the bags. But he is suddenly distracted by a figure who seems to have come out of nowhere. The passerby is tall, with blondish hair. His clothes are worn, a canvas bag hangs from his shoulder. His other arm is wrapped around a kind of package that Claudia can't quite make out.

The two men are talking, apparently about the package. The man who'd shown no sign of reading takes it in his hands, turns it this way and that. He discusses something briefly with the passerby, appears to come to an agreement, and slips his hand in the pocket of his jacket. As he removes his hand, something falls on the ground. To Claudia, the object looks like a small present. The passerby bends to pick up the object, hands it to the man, who thanks him and returns it to his pocket. Then the man who'd shown no sign of reading gives some money to the passerby, who bows slightly, politely, and as he departs, says something more. The man who'd shown no sign of reading looks again at the package, slips it under his arm, grabs hold of his suitcases, goes into the house, and closes the door behind him.

Claudia remains still for a moment, touched and surprised to have witnessed the return of the man who'd shown no sign of reading. Finally, she is filled with joy. As she leaves, she knows she will often recall this story. She's not sure how or why, but the man who'd shown no sign of reading has provided her with the stuff of dreams.

Carmen wakes up in the arms of Terry, who's resumed his reading after dozing a bit.

"Mmm . . . I feel better."

Terry puts his book down, cuddles her a little.

"You must've been tired, is all."

"Could be. It was like there was something all bottled up."

"There's times it's like that."

Terry continues to caress Carmen in silence.

Then: "If you ask me, we'd be better off staying here a couple of days, take things easy, then decide where it is we want to be going."

"Mmm . . ."

Terry interprets this response as positive.

"We might telephone back home, just to say where it is we are and find out how things are going back there."

"Mmm . . ."

"We might do a picnic by the water, just to hear the water."

"And the wind."

"And the wind."

Carmen squeezes closer to Terry.

"Do you think it'd be all right to sell the pin to buy some paintings? Back in Moncton, I mean."

"And why wouldn't it be all right?"

"Well, it was a gift, wasn't it?"

Terry thinks about this, thinks of the man who'd shown no sign of reading.

"Well, wasn't he a painter himself? Far as I'm concerned, it'd be a kind of tribute to him."

Terry continues to think, adds: "Might be we could even buy a big one from Yvon Gallant."

Carmen is enthused by the possibility.

"Do you really think so, then? You think we could buy three?"

"Could be. If we found the right person to sell the thing to. I heard of a fellow in Bouctouche knows a thing or two 'bout diamonds. One of the Duplessis clan, as I recall."

Terry can already see himself doing business with the fellow from Bouctouche.

"And one day, we'll be telling all this to the boy."

"Or girl."

"Or girl. Girl, boy, makes no difference."

Moving away or closer — though from or to what, he can't say — Hans thinks how much he enjoyed picking up and returning to the man with the suitcases the small, prettily wrapped box that had fallen to the ground. He enjoyed feeling the lack of weight of the gift in his hand, the feather-light present that felt unlike anything he could recall, as it absorbed the beauty of the day and crystallized everything. Hans also thinks he saw something far away shift in the eyes of the man just before he decided to buy the jigsaw puzzle of the winter landscape. And he thinks of his identity papers, which he still feels like throwing away.

How strange that neither you, my son, nor you, my wife — but who are you both really? — received the last tiny parcel of energy I was able to direct towards the earth. I thought surely you would be the ones it would reach, but no. Instead, this minute wavelength infiltrated a shop somewhere in an American city, I think — more and more, I'm losing all trace of it — and caused to slip into the hands of a young girl that music I loved so much, the *Orphaned Notes* — I can't even remember the composer, all air and wind. That slippage, that barely noticeable progression, was all I was able to manage, and really only because that young girl's hands were open.